✳✳✳✳✳✳✣ THE ✣✳✳✳✳✳✳✣

HISTORY
— OF —
INSULTS

THE HISTORY OF INSULTS

OF

INSULTS

OVER 100 PUT-DOWNS, SLIGHTS & SNUBS THROUGH THE AGES

COMPILED BY **NATHAN JOYCE**

Looks like a barrel border to me!

DOG 'n' BONE

This edition published in 2022 by Dog 'n' Bone Books
An imprint of Ryland Peters & Small Ltd

20–21 Jockey's Fields
London WC1R 4BW

341 E 116th St
New York, NY 10029

www.rylandpeters.com

Previously published in 2017

10 9 8 7 6 5 4 3 2 1

Text © Nathan Joyce 2017
Design © Dog 'n' Bone Books 2017

For picture credits, see page 112

A CIP catalog record for this book is available from the
Library of Congress and the British Library.

ISBN: 978 1 912983 56 8

Printed in China

MIX
Paper from
responsible sources
FSC® C106563
www.fsc.org

Designer: Jerry Goldie
Art director: Sally Powell
Head of production: Patricia Harrington
Publishing manager: Penny Craig
Publisher: Cindy Richards

Thou art as
loathsome as
a toad.

CONTENTS

INTRODUCTION

We know that the Ancient Greeks and Romans transformed the known world with their philosophy, culture, and technology, but it may be refreshing to learn that their pioneering innovations extended to insulting each other. It turns out that both Greek and Roman soldiers carved humorous messages into sling-shot balls before flinging them at their enemies. Some of the choice cuts include "Here's a sugar plum for you," "For Pompey's backside," and the rather timeless "Ouch!".

You, minion, are too saucy!

You lousy gongoozler!

Shakespeare contributed to literature more than any writer before or after him. It may surprise you, however, to find out that this unparalleled genius enjoyed a well-placed "Your mamma" gag like the rest of us, kindly leaving one for us to uncover in *Titus Andronicus*. He was not the first, though. He was passing on a torch that had been lit in Ancient Babylonia (around 1,500 BCE) by a cheeky student who alluded to an unknown mother's promiscuity. A significant moment in human civilization, for sure, but the "Your mamma" gag is trumped (I'm not even sorry—I'm contributing to a proud tradition) by an even more esteemed joke. That's right. Humanity's first contribution to written comedy was… a fart joke, dating back to 1,900 BCE. Alas, it wasn't "I fart in your general direction," just for the record.

Since then, civilizations have come and gone, but their glorious insults remain, undimmed. In the pages that follow, you'll find some of the finest burns in history, courtesy of the Vikings, Medieval French, Song Dynasty Chinese, Victorians, and the Jazz Age Americans, among others. You'll also find a smattering of the most extraordinary, unusual put-downs from across the world, which are still proudly used today. I doff my cap to the Japanese.

Go boil your shirt!

CHAPTER 1

CLASSICAL CURSES

Abuse from the Romans, Greeks, and Vikings.

TRANSLATION:
You absolutely reek!

TRANSLATION:
You are so insufferably dull that I may
actually die of boredom!

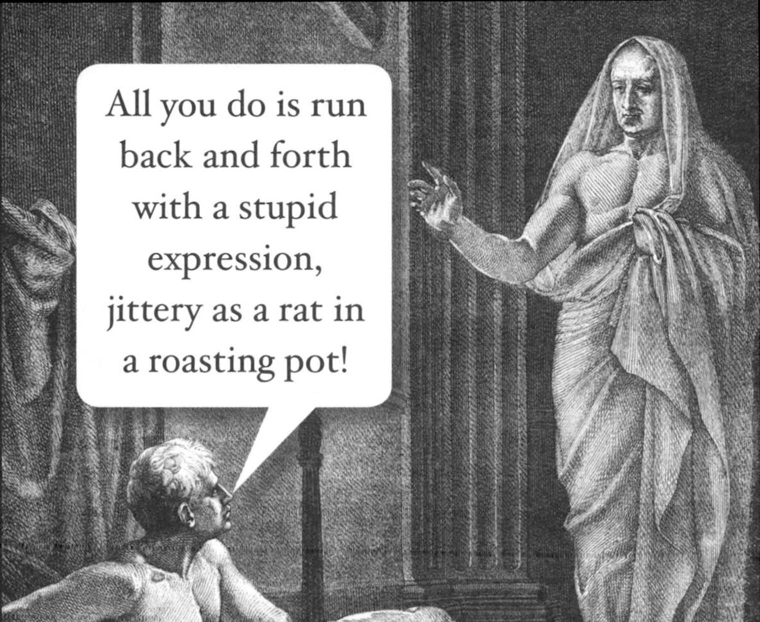

TRANSLATION:

You are a frantic, moronic waste of space!

14

TRANSLATION:
My word, his cheeks
are as pale
as they are chubby!

15

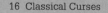

garlic, which remained from the many times she had broken wind, her hairiness which was more than that of a hedgehog, and the palm-fiber-like texture of her skin.

TRANSLATION:
An unholy stink emanated from her as a result of her uncontrollable urination and sustained farting, on top of her considerable hairiness and prickly skin.

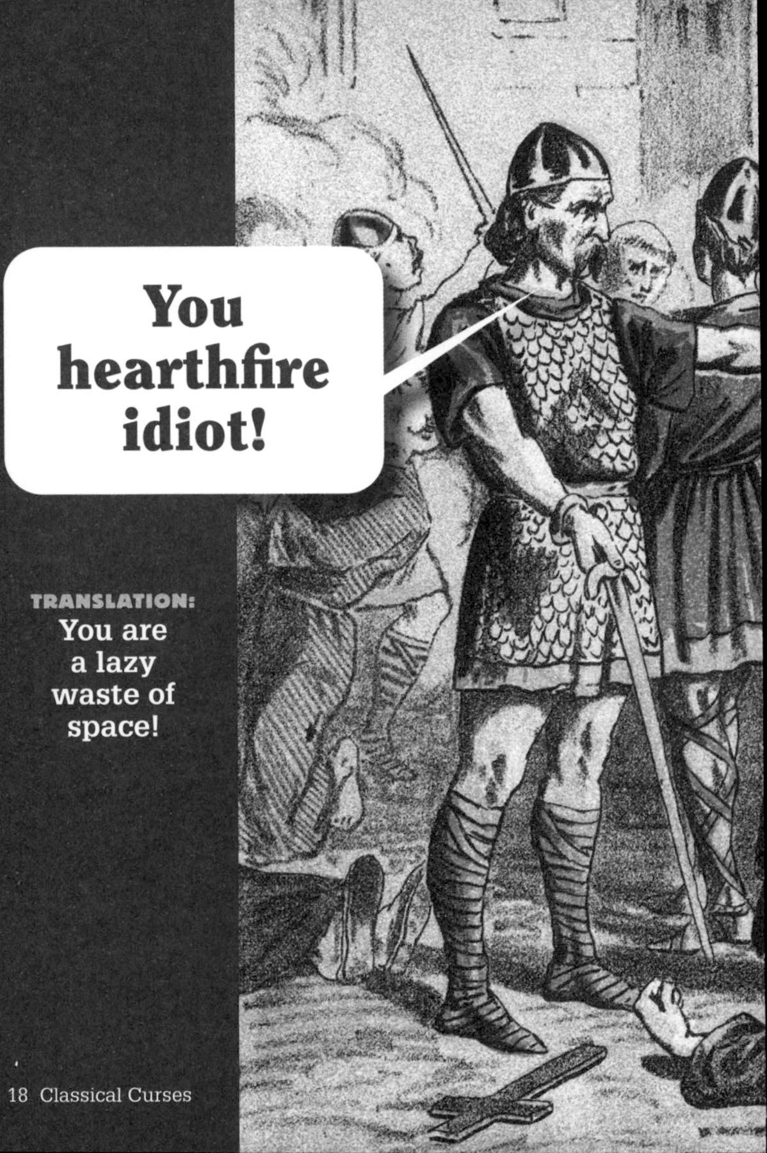

TRANSLATION:
You are a lazy waste of space!

You raven starver!

TRANSLATION:
You put up no fight, you coward!

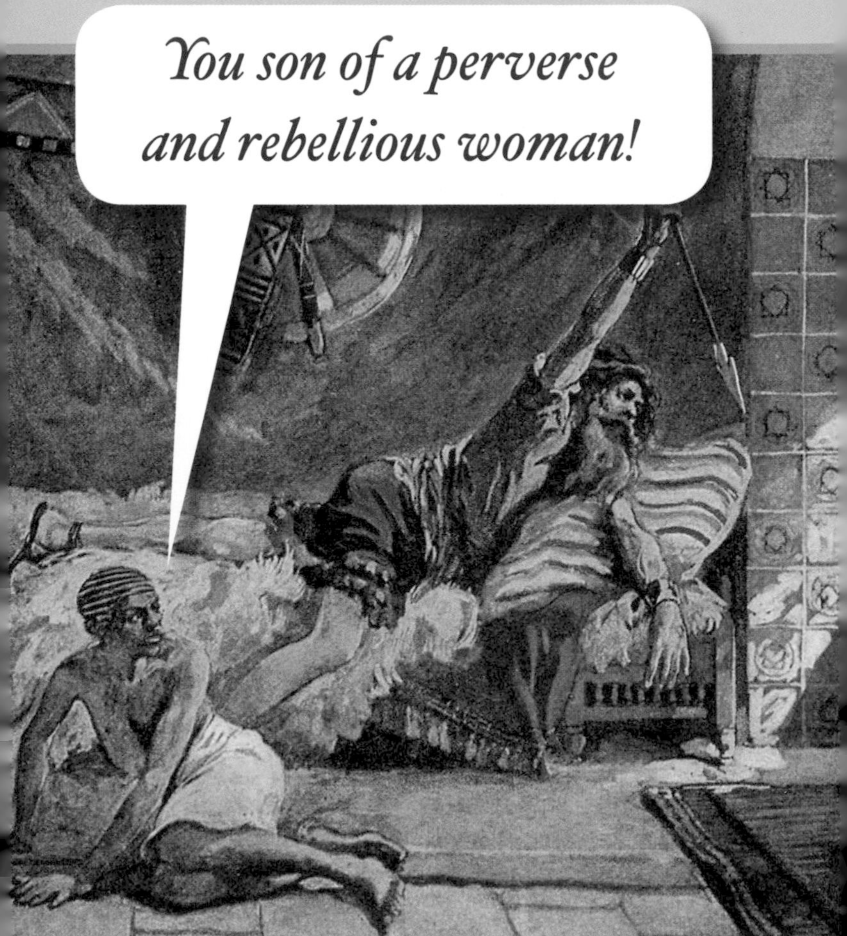
You son of a perverse and rebellious woman!

CHAPTER 2

BIBLICAL
BANTER

*Slander from the
scriptures.*

You son of a b***h!

Your nose is like the tower of Lebanon!

TRANSLATION:
You are one ugly chump!

24

You snakes! You brood of vipers!

TRANSLATION:
You crafty, treacherous jerks!

As a dog
returneth
to his vomit,
so a fool
returns to
his folly.

My little finger is thicker than my father's loins.

TRANSLATION:
I'm *ahem* a bigger man than my father.

Go and learn what this means!

TRANSLATION:
You will need to acquire some more gray matter before you can understand what I'm saying, you cretins!

Nazareth!
Can anything
good come
from there?

TRANSLATION:
I support Bethlehem FC and I'm proud
of it. Your town is a dump.

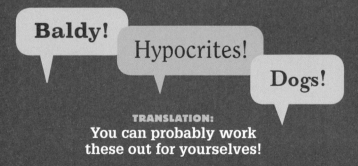

Baldy!

Hypocrites!

Dogs!

TRANSLATION:
You can probably work
these out for yourselves!

CHAPTER 3

MEDIEVAL MUD SLINGING

Norman French, Italian, and English invective.

TRANSLATION:
You greedy, sinful monster!

You've eaten farro soup!

TRANSLATION:
You loathsome commoner!

ROMEO und JULIA.
Nº 3. CAPULET stützt TYBALT, der von ROMEO verwundet.

Filthy worm head!

TRANSLATION:
You disgusting, deformed,
little creature!

Thou woldest make me kisse thyn old breech, And swere it were a relyk of a saint, Though it were with thy fundement depeint! But by the croys which that seint Eleyne fond, I wolde I hadde thy coillons in myn hond, In stride of relikes or of seintuarie, Lat kutte hem of…

TRANSLATION:
You would force me to kiss your old trousers and swear they were relics of a saint, even though they had been stained by your arse! But by the cross which Saint Helen found, I wish that I had your balls in my hand instead of relics. Let's cut them off!

By God… thy drasty rhyming is not worth a turd!

TRANSLATION:
Do shut up, you tiresome moron.

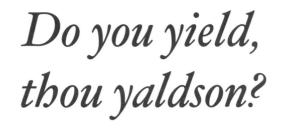

Do you yield,
thou yaldson?

TRANSLATION:
Do you surrender,
you son of a prostitute?

TRANSLATION:
Vengeance is mine, you classless scoundrel!

TRANSLATION:
Take this, you weak and ineffectual man!

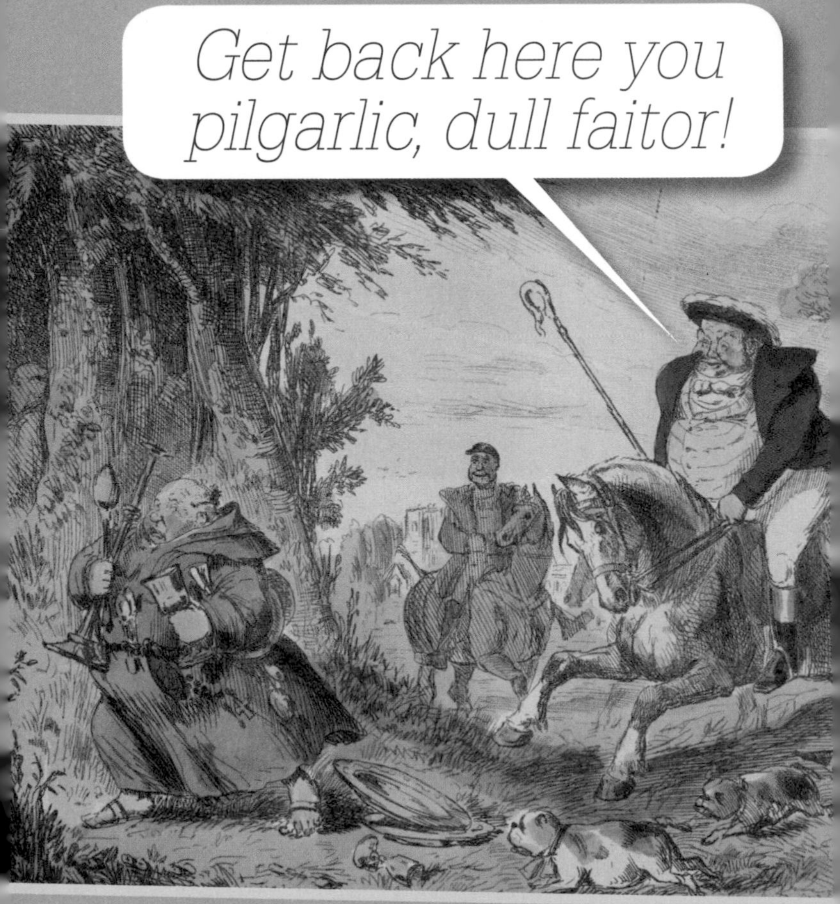
Get back here you pilgarlic, dull faitor!

CHAPTER 4

TUDOR AND SHAKESPEAREAN INSULTS

Some 16th-century slights.

TRANSLATION:
Come here, you bald,
fat traitor!

You have taken my wife as your leman, you rabbit-sucker. A pox upon you!

TRANSLATION:
So my wife is your mistress, you weasel. I wish you a painful death!

But I saw you with a laced-mutton yesterday— I thought you were a wittol!

TRANSLATION:
But I saw you with a call girl yesterday— I thought you were a contented cuckold!

Who are you calling fustilugs, you mooncalf!

TRANSLATION:
How dare you call me a fat and slovenly woman, you monstrous freak!

You, minion, are too saucy!

TRANSLATION:
You, hussy, are too insolent!

Thy tongue outvenoms all the worms of the Nile.

TRANSLATION:
Your breath is appalling.

Methink'st thou art a general offence and every man should beat thee.

TRANSLATION:
You are universally irritating and deserve a good hiding from everyone.

Thou art as loathsome as a toad.

TRANSLATION:
So you win the prize for being
simultaneously hideous and disgusting.

A weasel hath not such a deal of spleen as you are toss'd with.

TRANSLATION:
Not even a weasel
is as loathsome as you.

And he had the gall to call me a gorbellied flippertigibbet!

He had the nerve to call me a fat gossip-monger!

What a deboshed swinge-buckler!

What a drunken bully!

Thou art a base, proud, shallow, beggarly, three-suited, hundred-pound, filthy, worsted-stocking knave; a lily-liver'd, action-taking knave; a whoreson, glass-gazing, superserviceable finical rogue; one-trunk-inheriting slave; one that wouldst be a bawd in way of good service, and art nothing but the composition of a knave, beggar, coward, pandar, and the son and heir of a mongrel bitch.

TRANSLATION:
You are an utter butthead,
in every conceivable respect.

> An ass-head and a coxcomb and a knave, a thin-fac'd knave, a gull!

TRANSLATION:
You stupid, arrogant, dishonest, feeble fool!

Your brain is as dry as the remainder biscuit after voyage.

TRANSLATION:
There's not much going on upstairs with you.

He smells like a fish, a very ancient and fish-like smell.

TRANSLATION:
He sure is a whiffy chap.

You base football player!

TRANSLATION:
You're a lowly jock!

You have such a February face,
so full of frost, of storm
and cloudiness.

TRANSLATION:
Lighten up, you miserable wretch.

I do desire we may be
better strangers.

TRANSLATION:
I would dearly love to have nothing
to do with you—starting now.

Peace, ye fat guts.

TRANSLATION:
Arrivederci, porky!

You scullion.
You rampallian.
You fustilarian.
I'll tickle your
catastrophe.

Unterbeamter: „Sir John F

TRANSLATION:
You outrageous scoundrel.
I'll spank your backside for you.

" – Falstaff (zum Pagen): „Junge, sag'ihm, dass ich taub bin."

FALSTAFF (Heinrich IV.)

Siehe Rückseite.

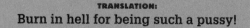

The devil damn thee black
thou cream-faced loon!

TRANSLATION:
Burn in hell for being such a pussy!

The devil
a puritan that he is,
or anything
constantly,
but a time-pleaser;
an affectioned
ass that cons state
without book
and utters it by
great swarths.

TRANSLATION:
He's nothing but a pompous flatterer;
a pretentious moron who thinks way too
much of himself.

> *How low am I,*
> *thou painted maypole?*

TRANSLATION:
Well if I'm short, then you're
a lanky, make-up-smothered show-off.

> No longer from head to foot
> than from hip to hip, she is
> spherical, like a globe, I could
> find out countries in her.

TRANSLATION:
She's really quite wide
(or possibly a Tudor "Yo mamma's
so fat...").

> **Sweep on, you fat**
> **and greasy citizens!**

TRANSLATION:
Get lost, you odious creatures.

TRANSLATION:
You deserve a beating, you dirty scoundrel. Don't ever say that my scrotum is longer than my penis!

My, he is a Crab Lanthorn.

TRANSLATION:
He's a mightily peevish fellow.

CHAPTER 5

19TH-CENTURY CHEAP SHOTS

19th-century Victorian English, Chinese, and French put-downs.

You must be dicked in the nob walking round these parts, you cockalorum.

There's no need to be such a sneaksby.

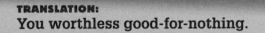

TRANSLATION:
You worthless good-for-nothing.

Fàntong!

TRANSLATION:
You are an utterly useless person!
(Literally: you are a rice bucket!)

Fàng nǐ
ma de gǒu
chòu pì.

TRANSLATION:
What you said is
bulls**t. (Literally:
release your mother's
dog's stinky fart!)

Au nom de la loi, je vous arête, puterelle.

TRANSLATION:
I am arresting you,
you filthy woman
of ill repute.

Vous êtes bête comme ses pieds, gros turbot farci!

TRANSLATION:
You are as thick as a plank,
you fat, stuffed turbot!

Chaps, I appear to be chimping merry. I'm off with the jammiest bit of jam!

He looks like he'll shoot the cat before he visits the doodle sack...

Here's a bunch of fives, you bracket-faced clodhopper!

TRANSLATION:
This fist is for you, you ugly lout!

Kiss my cooler you chuckle-headed, cribbage-faced zounderkite!

TRANSLATION:
Kiss my ass you pock-marked, stupid idiot.

You're coming with me, you Haymarket Hector. And enough of the bear-garden jaw!

TRANSLATION:
It's off to the cells with you, pimp!
And no more of the coarse language!

TRANSLATION:
Brown-noser!

You, sir, are a gentleman of four outs.

TRANSLATION:
You, my man, are without wit, without money, without credit, and without manners.

Plan of the Intended Canal

Report of the Engineer respecting the intended canal

Cruikshank s.p

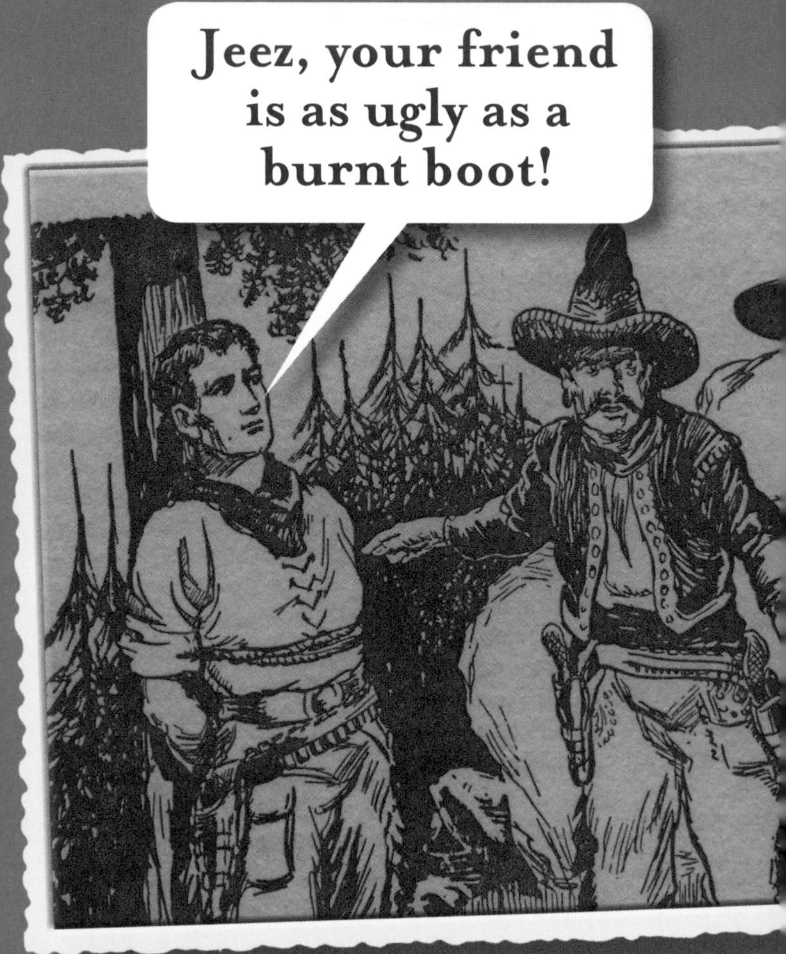
Jeez, your friend is as ugly as a burnt boot!

*

CHAPTER 6

WILD WEST WHIZZ-BANGERS

Cusses from cowboy country.

TRANSLATION:
Your associate is not aesthetically pleasing.

Stop being a coffee boiler and go play the California prayer book with those spooney spoops!

TRANSLATION:
Stop being a lazy oaf and go and play cards with those drunk fools!

But that sniptious whaler looks like a chiseler to me!

TRANSLATION:
But that big, vain guy looks like a cheat to me!

TRANSLATION:
Hey, fathead. Put your hands up or else you'll be lying on your backside in the dirt!

How about I pour us some Kansas sheep dip and we talk? You'll see that someone is telling tarradiddles about me.

TRANSLATION:
Why don't we have some sippin' whiskey and a chat? I think you'll find that some guy is telling tall tales about me.

That fella in the corner sure is lushington. He's airing the lungs like nobody's business.

TRANSLATION:
The chap in the corner is stinking drunk. He's swearing something rotten.

Looks like a barrel border to me.

TRANSLATION:
He looks like a down-and-out to me.

TRANSLATION:
I'm not a down-and-out (hiccup).
I'm the top dog in this joint.

Go boil your shirt!

TRANSLATION:
Get lost, sucker!

Hey — you better hobble your lip!

TRANSLATION:
You ought to shut up if you know what's good for you.

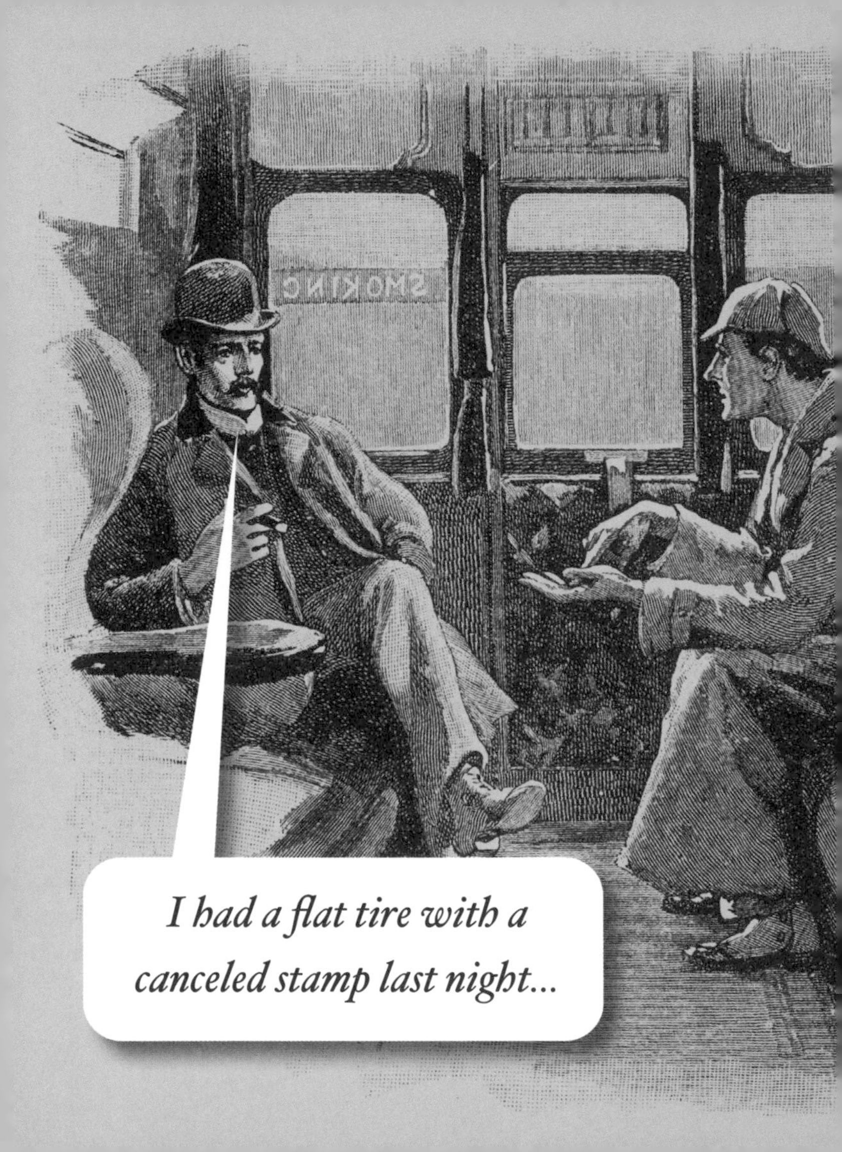
I had a flat tire with a canceled stamp last night...

CHAPTER 7

20TH-CENTURY BURNS

Taunts from the turn of the century.

TRANSLATION:
I had a disastrous date with a bashful woman last night…

SP

TRANSLATION:
You can get as dressed up as you like but you're still mutton dressed as lamb.

Stop casting a kitten. You're just upset because you were given the ice mitt last night.

TRANSLATION:
Stop having a strop. You're annoyed because you had your advances spurned last night.

You lousy gongoozler!

TRANSLATION: You bone-idle gawker!

I'd rather be a gongoozler than a spatherdab!

TRANSLATION:
Better that than a gossip-monger
and a blabbermouth!

You're nothing but a schlemiel!

TRANSLATION:
You're a clumsy loser!

Well at least I ain't no schmendrick!

TRANSLATION:
Yeah, well, you're a clueless mamma's boy!

You milky asterbar!

TRANSLATION:
You cowardly b**tard!

COCKNEY RHYMING SLANG

I fell on me bottle and glass when I was Brahms and Liszt!

TRANSLATION:
I fell on my a**e (glass)
when I was p**sed (Liszt = drunk).

That bloke's a right Hampton Wick.

TRANSLATION:
That guy is a right p**ck
(Hampton Wick).

I'm going to give that geezer a boot in the orchestras.

You're a pain in the Khyber.

He's Patrick Swayze!

✳

CHAPTER 8

CONTEMPORARY CURSES

Modern-day mockery from around the world

Kisama tama!

Japanese for "Lord of donkey balls."

TRANSLATION: I won't be writing you a Christmas card this year.

Chipkali ke gaand ke pasine.

Bengali for
"Sweat of
a lizard's ass."

TRANSLATION:
You loathsome, foul-smelling
creature.

Ek wens jou vingers verander in vishoeke, en jou balle begin te jeuk.

Afrikaans for
"I hope your fingers turn into fishing hooks and you get an itch in your balls."

TRANSLATION:
I wish you all the best in your future endeavors.

108 Contemporary Curses

Shattenparker!

German for
"A person who parks
in the shade!"

TRANSLATION:
You insufferable wimp!

Sanjam da prdnem na tebe!

Serbo-Croat for
"I dream about
farting on you."

TRANSLATION:
I'm going to get you back
SO badly.

Megi tröll hafa pína vini.

Icelandic for
"May the trolls take your friends."

TRANSLATION:
I will not be hurrying out to purchase you a wedding gift.

PICTURE CREDITS